LITTLE RED TRAIN
TO THE RESCUE

For Matthew and Andrew

A RED FOX BOOK: 978 0 099 69221 8
(From January 2007)
0 09 969221 X

First published in Great Britain by Julia MacRae 1997
Red Fox edition published 1998

13 15 17 19 20 18 16 14 12

Red Fox Books are published by Random House Children's Books,
61-63 Uxbridge Road, London W5 5SA,
a division of The Random House Group Ltd,
in Australia by Random House Australia (Pty) Ltd,
20 Alfred Street, Milsons Point, Sydney, NSW 2061, Australia
in New Zealand by Random House New Zealand Ltd,
18 Poland Road, Glenfield, Auckland 10, New Zealand
and in South Africa by Random House (Pty) Ltd,
Isle of Houghton, Corner Boundary Road & Carse O'Gowrie, Houghton 2198, South Africa

THE RANDOM HOUSE GROUP Limited Reg No. 954009
www.**kidsatrandomhouse**.co.uk

A CIP catalogue record for this book is available from the British Library.

Printed and bound in Singapore

LITTLE RED TRAIN
TO THE RESCUE

Benedict Blathwayt

Red Fox

One wet and windy day, Duffy
Driver lit the fire in the little red
train and collected three trucks
from the goods yard.

The trucks were soon loaded and Duffy Driver and the little
red train set off for Birchcombe village, high up in the hills.
Chuff-chuff, chuffitty-chuff...

But as they came round a bend, what did they see...

Animals on the line!
Duffy put on the brakes with a scree...eee...ch
and the little red train stopped just in time.

When the animals were back in the
farmyard, the little red train set off again.
Chuff-chuff, chuffitty-chuff...

But as they came round a bend, what did they see...

The river had flooded the road!
Duffy put on the brakes with a scree...eee...ch
and the little red train stopped just in time.

They rescued the passengers from the bus on
the bridge and the little red train set off again.
Chuff-chuff, chuffitty-chuff...
But as they came round a bend, what did they see...

The wind had blown down a tree!
Duffy put on the brakes with a scree...eee...ch
and the little red train stopped just in time.

Everyone helped to move the tree
and the little red train set off again.
Chuff-chuff, chuffitty-chuff...

But the track got steeper and steeper and
the little red train hotter and hotter until...

P O P! HISSSSS! The safety valve blew off the boiler!
Duffy Driver put on the brakes with a scree...eee...ch
and stopped to let the little red train cool down.

Up in the hills there was snow,
so they set off again more slowly.
Chuff-chuff-chuff, chuu...ff, chuff...itty-chu...ff...
But as they came round a bend, what did they see...

A great pile of snow was blocking the line!
Duffy put on the brakes with a scree...eee...ch
and the little red train stopped just in time.

They all helped to clear the snow
and the little red train set off again.
Chuff-chuff, chuffitty-chuff...

But as they came to the last stretch
of line what did they find...

The points had frozen!
The little red train went off the wrong way.
Duffy put on the brakes with a scree...eee...ch
and the little red train stopped just in time.

The signalman poured hot water on
the points and with a chuff-chuff,
chuffitty-chuff the little red train ran
on towards the station at Birchcombe...

POST OFFICE

Everyone was there to greet them.
Duffy Driver blew the whistle, whee...eee...eee
and put on the brakes with a scree...eee...ch and the
little red train stopped at the platform just in time.

The passengers climbed down and helped to unload the supplies...

and Duffy Driver was given a special tea by the postmistress.

Then Duffy got back into the driver's
cab and after he had blown the whistle,
whee...eee...eee, the little red train raced
back home. It was downhill all the way.

Chuffitty-chuffitty,

chuffitty-chuff...

Adventures of the Little Red Train:

The Runaway Train
0 099 38571 6
(Mini Treasure 0 099 40302 1)

Little Red Train to the Rescue
0 099 69221 X

Faster, Faster, Little Red Train
0 099 26499 4
(Mini Treasure 0 099 47566 9)

Green Light for the Little Red Train
0 099 26502 8

The Great Big Little Red Train
0 099 45597 8

The Little Red Train Jigsaw Book
0 091 89315 1

Adventures of the Little Red Train mini hardbacks box set
0 091 89374 7

Little Red Train Adventure Playset
0 091 79842 6